# Where are the leaves?

## Contents

Written by Mary Roulston

Illustrated by Szilvia Szakall

**Collins**

# What's in this book?

Listen and say 🎧①

flower

forest

fruit

It's winter in the UK. Tom and his mum are walking in the forest.

## Spring

In the spring, it's not cold. Leaves grow on trees. Grass and flowers grow on the ground.

Flowers grow on some trees, too.

Many birds make nests in the trees. Birds lay eggs.

Animals have babies.

Baby animals play in the spring.
Playing makes them strong and clever.

# Summer

In the summer, the days are hotter than in the spring.

The leaves on the trees are big now.
Some trees grow fruit. Insects go to the
trees. They are looking for food.

These baby birds are learning to fly.

The baby animals are getting big now. There is lots of food for them to eat in the summer.

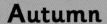

# Autumn

In the autumn, the days are shorter and it's colder than the summer.

Now the leaves on the trees are yellow, orange and red and they fall to the ground.

14

There are no flowers. Mushrooms are growing in the forest.

There are lots of leaves now.

Animals get ready for the winter.
They grow more fur. Some animals find
food and hide it.

Some birds fly to hotter places for the winter.

# Winter

In the winter in the UK, it is colder than in the autumn. Sometimes it is very cold.

Some trees haven't got any leaves, now.
Plants don't grow.

Some animals sleep a lot. They only wake up to find food.

We sometimes go out to play in the winter. We wear lots of clothes so we don't get cold.

# Picture dictionary

Listen and repeat

fur

grass

insects

leaf

mushroom

nest

**1** Look and match

spring    summer    autumn    winter

**2** Listen and say

# Collins

Published by Collins
An imprint of HarperCollins*Publishers*
Westerhill Road
Bishopbriggs
Glasgow
G64 2QT

HarperCollins*Publishers*
1st Floor, Watermarque Building
Ringsend Road
Dublin 4
Ireland

William Collins' dream of knowledge for all began with the publication of his first book in 1819.

A self-educated mill worker, he not only enriched millions of lives, but also founded a flourishing publishing house. Today, staying true to this spirit, Collins books are packed with inspiration, innovation and practical expertise. They place you at the centre of a world of possibility and give you exactly what you need to explore it.

© HarperCollins*Publishers* Limited 2020

10 9 8 7 6 5 4 3 2

ISBN 978-0-00-839664-0

Collins® and COBUILD® are registered trademarks of HarperCollins*Publishers* Limited

www.collins.co.uk/elt

British Library Cataloguing in Publication Data

A catalogue record for this publication is available from the British Library.

Author: Mary Roulston
Illustrator: Szilvia Szakall (Beehive)
Series editor: Rebecca Adlard
Commissioning editor: Fiona Undrill and Zoë Clarke
Publishing manager: Lisa Todd
Product managers: Jennifer Hall and Caroline Green
In-house editor: Alma Puts Keren
Project manager: Emily Hooton
Editor: Rebecca Adlard
Proofreaders: Natalie Murray and Michael Lamb
Cover designer: Kevin Robbins
Typesetter: 2Hoots Publishing Services Ltd
Audio produced by id audio, London
Reading guide author: Emma Wilkinson
Production controller: Rachel Weaver
Printed and bound by: GPS Group, Slovenia

Download the audio for this book and a reading guide for parents and teachers at www.collins.co.uk/839664

Collins **Peapod readers**

Reader level 4
CEFR Lower A1

## What do you know about the seasons?

Inspire a love of reading with stories that are written from a child's perspective and will encourage children to discover the world around them. With audio and activities, Peapod Readers are the perfect start to a child's journey into learning English.

- *Before and after reading activities*
- *Picture dictionary*
- *Exam practice for Cambridge Pre A1 Starters, working towards A1 Movers*
- *Reading guide online*

 **Download the audio at www.collins.co.uk/839664**

| Level | CEFR | Words in story | Headword count |
|-------|---------|----------|------|
| 1 | Pre A1 | 50–70 | 80 |
| 2 | Pre A1 | 100–140 | 200 |
| 3 | Pre A1 | 150–230 | 400 |
| 4 | Lower A1 | 250–500 | 670 |
| 5 | A1 | 650–950 | 820 |

Non-fiction

ISBN 978-0-00-839664-0

9 780008 396640 >

collins.co.uk/elt

⊜ POWERED BY COBUILD

# Where is she?

Deborah Friedland          Gustavo Mazali